Postman Pat and Jess are getting ready for work.

Pat and Jess set off in the van.

Mrs. Goggins is waiting for Pat at the Post Office.

Pat is loading the van. Jess is helping him.

Sam Waldron, the Reverend Timms and Miss Hubbard say hello.

Postman Pat arrives at the school.

The children run up to take the letters for Mr Pringle.

Postman Pat in on his way to Greendale.

Pat stops to help George Lancaster start his tractor.

The Thompsons are busy picking apples when Pat arrives.

Granny Dryden has a cup of tea ready for Postman Pat.

Peter Fogg is crossing the road with six sheep.

Jess counts them as they go by.

Pat has a very big parcel for Ted Glen.

At Greendale Farm Pat helps the twins to collect the day's eggs.

Mrs. Pottage sells Pat a dozen eggs.

When Pat gets back to the Post Office Dr. Gilbertson is posting a letter.